PROLOGUE:
THE RIVER REMEMBERS

Before the oil. Before the guns. There was only the river.

Tombia was once a quiet place.

The kind where the river told time better than any clock.

Where laughter rose from market stalls and drums echoed stories beneath moonlight.

Where silence meant peace — not fear.

But that was before the pipelines.

Before the air turned thick with smoke.

Before the boys picked up guns.

Before Nzali.

Long before all of that, there came the missionaries.

They arrived by boat — pale-skinned and sun-drenched, with crates of Bibles, vaccines, and good intentions. Among them were Maria's parents, idealistic volunteers from Europe, full of purpose and naivety. They brought their daughter with them — a quiet girl no older than eight, curious but timid, clinging to her mother's hand.

Tombia welcomed them with wary hospitality.

And for a while, it worked.

They set up a small clinic. Built a classroom. Taught hymns by lantern light. Maria would run between lessons and the chapel, her shoes always muddy, her voice just starting to grow bold.

Then the fevers came.

Malaria. Cholera. Dysentery.

Death crept into the huts like mist. The other missionaries panicked. They called for boats, packed their trunks, prayed quick and shallow prayers. And when the riverboats came for evacuation, Maria's parents left with the rest.

They were supposed to wait for her.

They didn't.

In the chaos, they assumed someone had taken her aboard.

No one had.

They left her.

Forgotten.

By accident or fear — it didn't matter.

The boats left.

And Maria remained, standing barefoot in the chapel doorway, watching the only people she knew vanish into the river mist.

Everyone else left — except for one.

Mother Elizabeth.

The oldest member of the mission team, Elizabeth was from England — her accent clipped, her hands creased, her back unbowed. While others brought sermons, she brought bandages. While others counted conversions, she counted coughs.

When the team fled, she stayed.

And when she saw Maria — small, stunned, forgotten — she simply opened her arms.

Maria stepped into them without a word.

Together, they survived the storm.

They buried the dead, fed the sick, lit candles in the night. Elizabeth didn't just tend to Maria. She raised her. Called her daughter. Taught her scripture, science, silence, and strength.

Years passed.

Elizabeth's hair turned white. Her hands shook. But Maria stood taller each season. She learned to pray over bodies without flinching. To mend wounds the world didn't see. She became Sister Maria, guardian of the mission, keeper of the flame.

When Elizabeth finally passed — quietly, in her sleep — Maria did not weep.

She simply rang the chapel bell twelve times.

Then lit a candle, and kept going.

But the world had not grown gentler.

Oil bled into the river.

Foreign suits bargained with chiefs.

Children disappeared into the forest and returned as rebels.

The boys she once taught began carving Nzali into the clay walls.

They came at night — for sanctuary, for silence, for blood.

Some said she should fear them.

Some said she helped them.

No one knew.

Maria just kept lighting candles.

And when the wind blew hard enough, she still heard Elizabeth's voice:

"To stay… is the hardest thing."

She'd whisper back:

"That's why we stayed."

Across the water, a canoe moved quietly through the mangroves.

Men in black.
Steel in hand.
Eyes cold with memory.

Nzali was coming.

It began not as rebellion, but as survival. A spark between orphans. A hunger shared by soldiers who once believed in nations and now believed in nothing but the creeks.

Priye Mazani remembered the mission school — the feel of chalk, the sting of hunger, the sermons no one listened to. Now he was commander, rifle in hand, silence in his soul. He moved like shadow. Thought like storm.

His brother, **Tonye**, was the opposite.

All flame.

All noise.

All edge.

Where Priye was restraint, Tonye was explosion. And people followed him not because they agreed — but because they feared where he would go without them.

They were forged by blood.

Tempered by betrayal.

And aimed by **Isabelle**.

Priye's wife wasn't the best fighter. But she didn't need to be. She was the strategist — the one who turned fury into plans, fists into leverage, and grief into currency. Her name was never chanted, but every successful ambush bore her design.

Their first strike came on a night heavy with rain. Dugouts pushed out from the island, gliding under banana leaves and fog. By dawn, a government depot lay emptied — oil drums gone, guards silenced, alarms bypassed. It was surgical. Clean. Deliberate.

And back in Tombia, the rumours began.

Not of criminals.

Of liberators.

Fishermen started sleeping with radios on. Mothers warned their sons to stay indoors. The king called a council.

It was a movement.

A reckoning.

A name carved into rusted rifles, whispered by barefoot recruits, and feared by kings.

Not everyone believed.

Not everyone followed.

But no one ignored them.

Some said it would end quickly.

That the army would crush it.

That the Americans would intervene.

That the river would swallow them like it did every other rebellion.

But the creeks don't kill what they raise.

They teach it to disappear.

To strike.

To wait.

And Nzali waited.

Because in the Niger-Delta, nothing stays buried.

The jungle regrows.

The water rises.

And the river —**the river remembers**.

*Though inspired by the situation in the Niger-Delta area of Nigeria, **Nzali: The Brotherhood** is a fictional story. Names, characters, places, and events are products of the author's imagination or are used fictitiously. Any resemblance to actual persons, living or dead, or to real events is entirely coincidental.*

CHAPTER 1:
THE FIRST STRIKE

The crude oil depot on the outskirts of Port Harcourt loomed like a rusted fortress in the dark, its tanks swollen with unrefined petroleum, pipelines coiled like snakes across cracked concrete. Halogen lights cast harsh white beams across the yard, creating long shadows and narrow corridors of visibility. The scent of oil, rust, and something ancient clung to the air — the kind of smell that never left your clothes.

In the shadows beyond the barbed wire perimeter, twenty men crouched. Their faces were painted with river clay, their movements honed by weeks of swamp drills. At the centre of them, Priye Mazani whispered into his handheld radio.

"Alpha team — on me. Bravo — flank right. No voices unless I say."

He lowered the device and turned to his brother.

"You sure about this?" he asked.

Tonye Mazani didn't answer immediately. The younger Mazani brother grinned, his white teeth flashing in the dark. His AK-47 rested across his shoulders like a farmer's hoe.

"We're past sure," Tonye said, spitting into the mud. "It's showtime."

Where Priye was controlled, Tonye was chaos. The younger brother's energy radiated through the group — nerves, yes, but also fire. He was the blood that kept Nzali aggressive, unpredictable. Priye, meanwhile, was the mind. And the weight of command wore heavier on him than his combat gear.

They moved.

Nzali's two-pronged approach was designed by Isabelle — Priye's wife, and the strategic mind behind the brotherhood's most precise strikes. The depot's perimeter sensors had been studied for weeks, guards' schedules cross-referenced, gate access routines exploited. Every inch of the assault was planned with a surgeon's precision.

The militants cut the first section of fence with bolt cutters wrapped in rubber and rags to deaden the sound. Inside, the depot's back lot opened like a maze — pipelines coiling through sludge, storage tanks glistening under the floodlights.

Priye's team split. Four peeled left toward the camera relay station. Two more took point, each armed with short-barrelled AKs and machetes for silent takedowns. Tonye led a squad toward the holding warehouse, where drums of crude stacked for export waited to be shipped.

They moved fast.

Guards were taken out with chokeholds and silenced blades. A pair of workers were rounded up near the pumps, duct tape slapped over their mouths, wrists bound with plastic ties. A field engineer tried to run. Tonye fired a single shot — a clean tap to the chest. The man dropped like a sack of grain.

"Clear the lanes!" Tonye barked. "Move those drums! Keep it quiet!"

They weren't there to destroy. Not yet. They were there to steal — to claim the oil, the wealth that had been robbed from their people for decades.

Priye entered the control room with two men at his side. The technicians inside froze, eyes wide. Priye raised his rifle, expression unreadable beneath his camo scarf.

"We're not here to kill," he said calmly. "We're here to collect what belongs to Tombia. Anyone touches an alarm, we clean this room first."

One man fainted on the spot. The others obeyed.

Outside, the forklifts rolled and steel drums were stacked onto trucks. The depot was being drained like a corpse.

A security vehicle blared to life on the main road.

"We've got movement!" one of the lookouts called.

Within seconds, Nzali's teams scattered to defensive positions.

Blue-and-white police trucks squealed into view, tyres spraying gravel. Sirens cried out like wounded dogs. A dozen armed officers spilled out, taking cover behind oil drums.

Tonye laughed.

"It's about time."

He hoisted a grenade launcher to his shoulder — an old Soviet RPG from the illegal arms cache Isabelle had sourced through a Cameroonian contact.

"You're early. Welcome to the Party!" he shouted.

The police opened fire.

That was enough for Tonye.

The rocket fired with a cough of smoke and flame, striking the blockade. A thunderclap followed — shrapnel, sparks, men flying.

Nzali's convoy surged through the breach. One of the trucks nearly flipped on a turn.

Inside the cabin, the young driver — Malik, barely twenty — kept his foot steady on the pedal, his hands shaking.

In the back, a fellow militant bled from a bullet graze but kept loading rounds into his rifle.

Priye's vehicle took the rear. He scanned the road behind them, watching as depot lights faded into the distance. His heart pounded. He'd taken lives before, but this felt different.

This was declaration.

Back at the creek compound — a concealed camp in the deepest part of the mangroves — Nzali's men were welcomed with cheers. Drums beat against barrels. Cook-fires roared. Women passed food, shouting praise.

That night, Nzali held a feast in celebration. Roast fish, yam porridge, palm wine. The young recruits danced. The older fighters laughed. The camp was alive with a hunger — not just for food, but for something deeper. Victory.

Isabelle stepped from her command hut, calm as always.

Her eyes found Priye in the crowd. He walked toward her, his face smudged with smoke, his chest heaving.

They embraced. Not with fire. But with relief.

"We're in business," he whispered into her ear.

"Now we find a buyer," Isabelle replied. "And expand. Tombia is only the beginning."

CHAPTER 2:

THE SUMMIT'S BLOOD

Nzali's creek camp hummed beneath the smothering heat of the Niger Delta. The air buzzed with insects, smoke, and the sharp scent of sweat and rusted metal. Militants moved in squads, rifles slung over shoulders, boots churning the mud as they drilled along the banks. Bamboo huts leaned over the water, patched together with tarp, zinc, and desperation.

Nzali had grown in both strength and legend. What began as a whisper in the mangroves was now a fire spreading across the swamps.

On the training field, Tonye Mazani strutted among the recruits — shirtless, lean, his skin glistening with oil and rain. He barked orders with the energy of a preacher and the madness of a storm.

"Reload faster, idiot. You fumble in a firefight, you're dead. Or worse, you get your brother killed."

The militants scrambled to obey, fingers trembling as they slammed magazines into rifles.

A scuffle broke out near the ammo shed — two recruits fighting over a handful of loose naira notes. Fists flew. Someone drew a knife.

Tonye didn't hesitate. He fired his rifle once into the air. The shot cracked like thunder, silencing the entire camp.

Then, without a word, he raised the barrel again and shot both men in the leg. The camp froze.

The wounded men cried out, writhing in the mud.

"We don't fight our own," Tonye shouted. "Our war is with Abuja. Not each other."

He slung the AK-47 over his shoulder and walked away, boots squelching in the muck.

From the command tent, Priye Mazani watched everything. He said nothing, but his face was drawn, his fingers clenched into fists at his sides.

"He's becoming reckless," he muttered.

"He's always been reckless," came Isabelle's voice behind him.

"You just used to think it was useful."

She stepped beside him, arms folded, black headscarf tucked beneath a weathered cap. Her eyes were cool, calculating — the same eyes that had mapped oil depots, bribed customs officers, and turned a militia into a movement.

"The men fear him now," Priye said. "Fear and loyalty are not the same."

"But they often work together," Isabelle replied.

Later that night, the planning team gathered around a warped table covered in maps, rig schematics, and satellite photos.

"We hit the refinery," Priye announced. "Not to destroy it. To cripple it. Shut it down and send a message."

The team nodded. Malik, a former pipeline technician turned Nzali lieutenant, tapped a pipeline sketch.

"Entry through the east drainage. It's shallow at low tide."

Isabelle leaned over the map with a red pen.

"That's where we place the charges. But not too much. Damage control valves only — we want the system offline, not the town in flames."

She circled fallback routes, timing windows, and exit plans. It was surgical. It was hers.

Tonye arrived late, still riding the adrenaline from the training yard. He didn't sit.

"I've got something to handle first," he said, eyes glittering. "An informant in Lagos has a lead — a possible buyer for our consignment."

Isabelle's eyes narrowed.

"What kind of lead?"

"money, ammunitions, everything we need. Need to check him out - see if he's legit!"

Priye hesitated.

"You're going alone?"

"I'll take two men. Quick in, quick out."

"Keep it clean."

Tonye grinned — the kind of grin that had gotten them into trouble since they were boys.

"Clean enough."

He left the next morning in a small private plane.

What he didn't know was that it was a trap.

The informant had arranged the meeting on Banana Island — the glitzy heart of Lagos wealth. Tonye and two of his men posed as logistics consultants, arriving in plain clothes by air and blending into the chaos of the city. Their destination was a luxury hotel hosting a regional oil investment summit.

The buyer never showed. Because there was no buyer.

State Security Service agents were already inside the hotel. The informant had flipped, selling Tonye's name in exchange for a government contract.

At the first sign of betrayal, Tonye didn't panic. He acted.

Disguised as kitchen staff, he and his men slipped into the banquet wing with a catering cart — two crates loaded with suppressed pistols, machetes, and two short-barrelled rifles.

Inside the ballroom, diplomats and oil executives clinked glasses and applauded a speaker on stage.

Then chaos erupted. Tonye fired first — a single shot into the chandelier. Screams filled the room.

His men moved with precision, cutting down targets while guests scrambled beneath tables. Tonye leapt onto the dais, kicked over the podium, and grabbed the informant — now cowering near the dessert table.

"You sell lies to Nzali?"

He didn't wait for an answer.

One bullet. Then another.

The massacre was brutal. Dozens injured. At least nine confirmed dead — including the visiting trade attaché of the Republic of Benin.

By the time hotel security and SSS operatives reacted, Tonye and his men were already gone — fire exits, back corridors, motorcycles staged behind the alley.

He left a note pinned to a wall:

"Nzali does not negotiate with liars."

At the creek camp, Priye stared at a static-filled TV as the headlines exploded across national news.

TERROR AT SUMMIT — NZALI CLAIMS DEADLY ATTACK IN LAGOS.

Isabelle sat beside him, arms crossed.

"He's gone too far," she said.

"He's my brother."

"And now, he's made us enemies of the world."

Tonye returned to camp just before dawn, blood on his shirt, still wearing the kitchen apron.

He tossed a gold wristwatch onto the table — one of the dead man's spoils.

"No more buyers backing out now."

Priye didn't answer. He hit Tonye square in the jaw.

They crashed into the planning table — fists flying, years of tension boiling to the surface. Maps scattered. Pens snapped. Oil-stained paper tore.

Outside, the camp froze. Recruits and officers gathered in silence.

Isabelle stepped between them and shouted:

"Enough!"

She glared at both men.

"You are brothers. Not enemies."

Tonye spat blood and shook his head.

"If he can't handle how we make progress, maybe he's not the one to lead."

"And if you can't follow orders," Priye growled, "you're a liability."

Silence.

Then Isabelle cut through it.

"They fear us now," she said.

"So we use that fear."

CHAPTER 3:
THE RIVAL'S HEAD

The mangroves whispered just before dawn, their stillness pierced by the sputter of outboard engines slicing across the creek. Mist clung low over the black water, wrapping Nzali's camp in a gauze of silence and sweat.

Then — gunfire. It came sharp and sudden, echoing like thunder-cracks between the palms. The sentry at the west watch-post dropped, blood misting the air.

"Intruders!" someone screamed from the shadows.

"We're under attack!"

Chaos erupted. Boats skidded to shore, heavy with rival militants — some in camo, others in torn jeans and bandoliers, all armed and howling. These weren't government troops. They were Otu-Rugo boys — a smaller militia from a rival Delta community, hired muscle trying to stake their own claim in Nzali's rising empire.

They'd picked the wrong morning.

Priye Mazani burst from his tent, rifle already cocked. He scanned the tree line and barked orders.

"Delta line! Defend the ridge! Ebi — flank with Team Bravo!"

Shots cracked from the mangroves.

Nzali militants scrambled to defensive positions, returning fire with disciplined bursts. Some fired from the rooftops. Others darted through huts, cutting through invaders with machetes.

The creek turned red. Mud sucked at boots. Bullets sang. Grenades tore through palm fronds.

Isabelle, barefoot and calm, stood on a raised platform behind the supply hut with binoculars in one hand and a pistol in the other. She wasn't just watching — she was commanding. Her voice cut through the confusion.

"They're pushing the south entrance! Redirect Team Echo! If they get past the boats, we're exposed!"

Jo, the older militant with a lined face and quiet rage, emerged from his quarters swinging a rusted machete. He struck one of the invaders across the face and dragged another into the water, drowning him as gunfire exploded above their heads.

Tonye arrived late, shirtless again, grinning like a lunatic.

"I missed breakfast, and you bring me a war? Bless you, boys."

He waded into the fight like a man welcoming a storm.

Fifteen minutes later, it was over. Bodies littered the mud. The scent of cordite and blood thickened the air.

The Otu-Rugo gang had been crushed — what remained of them fled into the swamp, leaving their dead behind.

Nzali suffered losses too. Four men killed, nine wounded. One was just sixteen.

Priye stood over the corpses, his breath ragged, his fists clenched.

"Bury our dead. Throw theirs in the creek."

Tonye, face smeared with mud and blood, pulled something from one of the rival leader's bodies.

It was a ring — signet-stamped, proof of identity.

"Okoro," he confirmed. "Their so-called 'warlord.'"

He turned to Priye.

"Let's make an example."

Later that afternoon, Nzali patrols carried a macabre message into the heart of Tombia.

In the middle of Okigwe Market, where vendors once hawked smoked fish and children played in puddles, a pole was hammered into the cracked earth.

Atop it: Okoro's severed head. Flies buzzed. Shoppers gasped and scattered.

Some wept. Some stared. No one touched it. Everyone understood. Nzali didn't share power.

Sister Maria was walking through the market when she saw it. She froze. The familiar scent of fish was drowned in copper and rot. She couldn't look away. Okoro's eyes — empty, gaping — seemed to follow her as she passed. A child tugged at her hand, asking what it meant. She had no answer, only memories.

She remembered Tonye being scolded for stealing mangoes — Mother Elizabeth shaking her head, telling him, "Strength without mercy makes a tyrant."

That boy had become a man of blood.

In Abuja, a closed-door security meeting descended into fury.

The President slammed a fist onto the mahogany table.

"Enough. Tombia is a cancer."

An airstrike was proposed.

A U.N. envoy pushed back — not yet. Not without a ground investigation. Not with civilians still trapped in the region.

International eyes were now fully on Nzali.

They weren't just a local uprising anymore.

They were destabilising oil markets, drawing in foreign policy hawks, and turning the Delta into a tinderbox.

Back in Tombia, in the crumbling royal palace with broken shutters and vines crawling up stone pillars, King Emekuku sat in silence.

He had seen the footage.

The rival's head.

The market's panic.

The loss of control.

His chiefs gathered around him, whispering, but he barely heard them.

"They were boys," he murmured. "Orphans in this very courtyard. I scolded them once for breaking into the shrine. Now…"

He reached for the wooden idol on the floor — his father's, passed down through four generations. It trembled in his grip. So did he.

"Now they rule. And I... I beg for relevance."

One of the younger chiefs knelt beside him.

"Your Majesty, we must act."

But Emekuku said nothing. He stared out the window at the darkening sky.

CHAPTER 4:
THE KING'S RETRIBUTION

The midday sun bled across the Niger-Delta like a wound. Its heat pressed down on Nzali's creek camp, thickening the air with the scent of sweat, mud, and scorched gunpowder. A metallic taste clung to every breath, as if the very earth remembered the blood spilled days earlier.

The camp had barely buried its dead from the Otu-Rugo ambush when Tonye started pushing for vengeance.

He paced outside the command tent like a caged panther, his left side still wrapped in a blood-soaked bandage. He hadn't slept. He hadn't stopped moving.

"That ambush was too precise," he muttered. "Too clean. Someone tipped them off."

He turned to Priye, eyes burning.

"It was the king. Emekuku. That coward sits on his throne while our boys bleed in the dirt."

Priye said nothing. He sat hunched over a table covered in maps, reports, and radio logs. The lines blurred before his eyes. His fingers trembled against the wood. He hadn't slept much either.

"We don't know that," Priye said finally. "If we strike him without proof, we lose the people."

Tonye slammed his hand against the table.

"The people don't care who rules them. They care who feeds them. Who protects them. Right now, that's us."

"And if you're wrong?"

"Then we kill a coward king. No great loss."

Isabelle entered quietly, her boots caked with mud, her expression unreadable.

"We can't afford to hesitate," she said, arms folded. "The attack exposed our position. We need to reassert dominance. Quickly."

Priye stood slowly. His face was unreadable, but his voice was tight.

"Fine. We hit him. But no unnecessary blood. No market massacres. No burned shrines. We don't want Tombia to fear us. Not yet."

At sunset, Tonye gathered ten of his most trusted militants. They loaded weapons into boats — AKs, grenades, machetes. Geared in camouflage uniforms — a clenched fist gripping a machete — sewn into armbands.

The boats drifted from the creek into the wider river like shadows.

The palace wasn't what it once was.

King Emekuku's home, once the pride of Tombia, now looked like a museum left to rot — cracked marble steps, chipped statues of old kings, faded portraits curling in the heat.

The guards were underpaid and undertrained. Half were asleep.

Nzali struck fast. They flooded the palace in minutes. Gunshots echoed off stone walls. Servants screamed and scattered. The few guards who resisted were dropped with clean headshots. Tonye walked straight through the carnage like a general in a storm.

He found Emekuku cowering behind a carved throne.

The king's robe was wrinkled. His eyes were wild.

"**Onye eze, ndi-gi nēkele gi**" Tonye said in his native language, igbo.
[offering greetings]

"You… you can't do this," Emekuku stammered. "I am the King, have you gone mad?"

Tonye silenced him with a backhand.

"It's you who has gone mad - sending amateurs to attack us."

Then he ripped the beaded crown from Emekuku's head and wore it.

"We, are the kings now, your gods - If this ever happens again, we will burn down this palace, with you in it"

But the king's humiliation wasn't complete. From one of the palace bedrooms, a cry rang out.

Emekuku's daughter — seventeen, terrified — was dragged from her room by two Nzali men. She fought. Screamed.

Tonye watched, unmoved.

"Bring her. She'll remind the people who's in charge."

The girl kicked and thrashed, her wrists bound with torn silk, her white dress stained with sweat and fear.

She was shoved into the back of a truck, still screaming as the engines roared to life.

On their way out of the village, the convoy ran into someone unexpected.

Sister Maria had been on her way to the palace to speak with the king — hoping to broker peace after Nzali's latest display in Okigwe Market.

Instead, she found herself standing in the road, her rosary in one hand, her mouth dry.

Tonye's truck braked in front of her. Dust swirled. The militants tensed.

And then Tonye stepped down, grinning.

"Look who walks with angels."

Sister Maria didn't flinch.

"You're a nuisance, Tonye," she said. "You're tearing Tombia apart."

He took a step closer. Sweat rolled down his temple. Blood had dried under his fingernails.

"Then marry me, Sister," he said. "Save my soul."

Maria didn't blink.

Tonye's smile faded, just a flicker. Then he climbed back into the truck and waved them forward. The convoy rolled on.

Behind them, Sister Maria knelt in the dust and whispered a prayer through clenched teeth.

Tonye and his men didn't stop at the palace.

As they exited the village, they swung by the local police outpost — a hollow shell of colonial pride with peeling paint and busted radios.

They torched it. Threw Molotovs through the windows and sprayed bullets through the doors.

Inside, three officers burned alive. Their screams were swallowed by the fire.

In the palace, King Emekuku collapsed beside his throne. The crown was gone. His daughter was gone. His guards were dead. His people would never follow him again.

"I promised peace," he whispered to the empty room. "Now I beg for mercy."

His chiefs stood in silence, powerless, watching their monarch break.

CHAPTER 5:
THE FOREIGN HAND

The compound in Port Harcourt bristled with steel and silence.

It wasn't a Nigerian military base. It was cleaner, colder — a repurposed international logistics hub now crawling with American contractors, satellite uplinks, encrypted radios, and biometric locks. It belonged to the Joint Task Force — a U.S.-backed coalition of special operatives and Nigerian intelligence tasked with one goal:

Crush Nzali.

Inside the operations tent, lit in sterile white, Steven "Hawk" Caldwell hunched over a drone feed from the Delta.

He was all muscle and scar — the kind of man who wore his past like a second skin. Former Navy SEAL.

Veteran of Kandahar, Fallujah, and Mogadishu. A survivor of missions that never made the news.

"Their movements are scattered," he muttered to his second-in-command, Carson. "They're fast. Fluid. Guerrilla precision."

Carson, ex-MARSOC, nodded.

"Classic swamp insurgency. But they're escalating."

"Yeah," Hawk growled. "And it's only going to get worse."

Across the table sat Nosa Badmus — director of Nigerian special operations, young for his rank, sharp-eyed, and fiercely nationalistic.

"We don't need cowboy tactics," Nosa warned. "This isn't Kandahar."

"No," Hawk said. "It's more personal. And the terrain's theirs."

Sitting between them was Henry Ofili — a tactical analyst with roots in both worlds: U.S.-trained, Nigerian-born, and fluent in the codes of both governments. He was the calm in the storm.

"We need movement maps. Fuel lines. Boat manifests. Then we strike clean," Henry said.

Back in Nzali's creek camp, word had reached Isabelle that foreign eyes were now on them. She was in the comms hut, thumbing through a decrypted message from one of her Port Harcourt informants. The note was brief:

Americans in-country. Task Force fully operational. Eyes above. Boots soon.

She burned the paper in a steel basin. No reaction. Just confirmation.

Later that night, in the quiet of the planning tent, she met with Priye.

"We need to think wider," she said, unrolling a local surveillance map. "If they're watching the Delta, we'll need foreign influence, better fire power, buyers. Offshore routes. Insulated paths."

Priye stared at the map.

"What about Kabor?"

Kabor was one of theirs — a seasoned mole inside the Nigerian offshore oil sector. Officially, he still worked for the government on contract, helping supervise production platforms. Unofficially, he remained loyal to Nzali.

"He's still embedded," Priye continued. "Still moving between rigs. Reach out to him. Tell him we need an international buyer. Quiet. Experienced."

Isabelle nodded once, then left the tent.

The next evening, as dusk settled over the mangroves, a commotion stirred near the camp's edge.

Jo, one of the senior militants, approached the command hut with a folded note sealed in plastic. It had been tucked beneath the fuel drums — no one saw who left it.

Isabelle took the note and read it.

Will connect soon. Buyer likely. Offshore. Will advise. — K

She handed the slip to Priye, who read it, then slid it into his pocket without a word.

Three nights later, Priye and Isabelle were planning their next major operation when a panicked runner burst into camp.

"Sir—Tonye's gone."

"Gone where?"

"He took five men. Hit a crude pipeline along the eastern corridor."

Priye's jaw clenched.

Isabelle's eyes narrowed.

"He did what?"

It was true.

Tonye had acted without orders, determined to prove himself.

He and a small squad had tracked a vulnerable section of the national pipeline network — one of the feeder lines near a government depot. His plan? Tap it, siphon barrels of crude, and sell them to a rogue dealer in Warri.

No coordination. No exit plan. Just fire and impulse.

The JTF was already airborne when Tonye set his charges.

Their surveillance network picked up heat signatures around the pipeline just before dawn. A customs drone confirmed movement — armed men, no I.D.

Hawk didn't wait.

"Saddle up. We move now."

By the time Nzali's men had punctured the pipeline and began filling crude drums into a makeshift boat, the first wave of helicopters screamed overhead.

Tonye's men opened fire immediately — desperate, cornered. They never stood a chance.

A gunfight erupted in the tall reeds and red mud.

Bullets flew. Trees splintered. Smoke swallowed the shoreline.

Within twelve minutes, all five militants were dead.

Except Tonye. He tried to run. Leaping over a chain-link fence at the depot's southern wall, he landed wrong.

A sickening crack shot through his ankle.

He collapsed in the mud, choking on pain. He tried to crawl, didn't get far.

By the time the SEALs reached him, he was curled against the fence, pistol half-buried in sludge, his face a grimace of fury and shame.

Hawk approached, rifle steady.

"Don't move."

Tonye looked up, defiant even in pain.

"You're late."

He surrendered.

Back at camp, the radio crackled just after dawn.

Isabelle stepped into Priye's tent.

"They've taken him."

Priye looked up.

"Tonye?"

She nodded once.

"JTF custody. He's not coming back."

Priye's breath caught.

He said nothing for a long time.

Then, slowly, he shook his head, in disappointment.

"He's an idiot, but we need to get him out….somehow!"

"Any word from Kabor yet?"

Isabelle handed him another slip — received that morning.

Buyer confirmed. American. Former expat. Name: Albert Dimitri. Coordinates and payment plan to follow.

Priye's eyes narrowed. The name meant nothing to him yet.

But this — this was the next chapter.

A brother gone.
A deal rising.
And a storm just over the horizon.

CHAPTER 6:
THE TRIAL AND THE BETRAYAL

Port Harcourt's courthouse swarmed with tension.

Barricades lined the streets. Armed officers flanked the courthouse steps. Crowds gathered behind yellow tape — reporters, activists, families of the slain, and curious bystanders drawn to the circus of justice.

Inside the tall colonial building, air conditioning hummed over the click of cameras and the rustle of note pads. News drones hovered above, transmitting every angle to a country — and a world — on edge.

Because today, **Tonye Mazani** — Nzali's lightning rod, the face of their most brutal attack — stood trial.

He limped into the courtroom, his hands cuffed, ankle in a brace, orange detainee shirt draped over his thin frame. Still, his chin was high. His eyes swept the gallery like he owned it.

Outside, the crowd was a mix of fury and awe.

Placards read:

"WE DEMAND JUSTICE!"
"NO PLACE FOR TERRORISM"
"FREE TOMBIA FROM NZALI!"

Inside, Tonye flashed his trademark grin at the judge.

"Good to see we all showed up on time."
His lawyer winced.

What few knew — including the prosecution — was that the trial was a formality. The real decision had already been made.

The plea deal had been accepted the night before — quietly, behind closed doors, under threat of A death sentence. In exchange for his cooperation, Tonye would hand over intel on Nzali's inner operations, their weapons caches, recruitment routes, enablers and contacts.

Tonye couldn't face death! Tough on the outside, a coward inside.

Back in the creek camp, Priye stood under the leaking roof of the comms tent, listening to the court broadcast over a crackling radio.

When the news broke — that Tonye had accepted a plea bargain — something inside him ruptured. He turned away.

His brother — his fire, his war mate, his last tether to family — had folded.

The camp was silent that day.

Not even the birds sang.

Isabelle, however, was composed.

When the message came — confirmed through a source at the Ministry of Justice — she didn't flinch.

Instead, she summoned her assistant, Ebi.

The bald and wiry young woman with Nzali tattoo beneath her collarbone stepped into the shadows of Isabelle's command tent.

"You called?"

Isabelle handed her a small vial.

"It's fast. Quiet. Enough to stop a heart."

Ebi looked down at the poison.

"Is this for…?"

"Tonye betrayed Nzali. You know what has to be done."

"Priye—"

"Can never know."

Ebi hesitated. Then nodded.

"When?"

"Tomorrow. As he arrives in court. Press crowd will cover your exit."

The next morning, the street outside the courthouse was even more crowded than before.

Security doubled.

Tonye's transport van pulled to a halt just past 9:00 a.m. Two guards flanked him, walking him up the stairs. He was shackled. Bruised. But breathing.

Then it happened.

In the commotion, a female journalist bumped into Tonye as he reached the top of the stairs. No one noticed the needle.

No one saw the sharp inhale.

By the time he turned to call out, his knees had buckled. He fell backward. Hard. A spasm shot through his limbs. Foam filled his mouth. The crowd screamed. Cameras clicked wildly. Within seconds, medics rushed in, but it was too late.

Tonye Mazani was dead before he hit the pavement.

Ebi was already gone — blending into the chaos, camera slung over her shoulder, press badge vanishing into a side alley.

Back at the creek, Priye collapsed to his knees as the radio confirmed it.

Not the plea.

Not the betrayal.

The death.

His brother — the wild flame of Nzali — was gone.

Later that night, Priye stood at the edge of the creek, Tonye's old knife in his hand. The blade was chipped, dull — a relic from their earliest days. He remembered Tonye holding it up when they were kids, declaring he'd never be ruled by anyone again.

"We'll be kings," Tonye had said.

Now he's dead!

Priye didn't cry.

He didn't speak.

But something inside him fractured.

Isabelle watched from her tent, expression still, jaw tight. She'd made the choice - for Nzali, for survival. But she didn't sleep that night. Not well.

In the JTF compound, Steven "Hawk" Caldwell studied the drone footage of the courthouse scene.

"There," said Henry Ofili, pointing at a freeze-frame of the female journalist brushing against Tonye.

"Tattoo on her shoulder. Nzali sigil. That's one of theirs."

Nosa Badmus swore under his breath.

"They killed him. It's insane - he was one of their leaders."

"That's their operative," Hawk muttered.

"And that's our lead."

He pinned the image to the intel board, right beside photos of Isabelle and Priye.

Nzali had just revealed something important.

They didn't forgive betrayal.
Not even family.

CHAPTER 7:
FIRE REBORN

The rains came early that morning. Heavy, unrelenting — soaking Nzali's creek camp until the mud swallowed boots and palm roofs sagged with water. But even in the downpour, Nzali's warriors trained.

Grief had a schedule now. And the war waited for no one.

At the edge of the camp, Priye Mazani stood alone beneath a corrugated overhang, Tonye's old knife in hand. The chipped blade felt heavier than usual, as if it remembered blood.

He hadn't slept in two nights.

A candlelight vigil was held for Tonye. A line of flames along the water. A silence too deep for words. Nzali mourned. But only Priye bled on the inside.

And Isabelle… she didn't cry.

She stepped in.

Not as a coup. Not even as ambition. But necessity.

While Priye drifted through camp like a ghost, Isabelle tightened patrol schedules, reassessed the caches, and brokered a regional alliance with smaller Delta factions who were willing to trade loyalty for arms and protection.

"They need order," she told Ebi one night.

"And Priye… Priye needs time."

Ebi nodded but said nothing. The young militant's face had grown harder since the courthouse. Her eyes lingered on Priye whenever he passed — but she never spoke to him. Not anymore.

Nzali was evolving. Under Isabelle's hand, it became sharper. Leaner. Less about spirit, more about strategy. She ran psychological drills with the new recruits.

Reinforced loyalty. Taught them how to lie with a straight face and how to kill without flinching.

The men whispered. Some missed Tonye's fire. Others feared Isabelle's precision. But no one doubted her.

As they occasionally did, Isabelle organised a shipment of food and medical supplies, drop off at the shores of Tombia. Flour, rice, garri, salt, canned fish, formula and other supplies — each bag stamped with Nzali's emblem.

Cheers erupted.

Meanwhile, back at the creek, Priye's suspicion of Isabelle grew. He watched her differently. He didn't ask about Tonye's death. But the suspicion grew. And when he saw Ebi that week — quiet, alert, avoiding him at all costs — the doubt turned to certainty.

One morning, he approached her by the ammo crates.

"You were at the courthouse," he said, voice low.

"Did you kill him? Did Isabelle get you to do it?"

Ebi didn't meet his gaze.

"Do what?"

"Answer me, did you kill Tonye?"

She turned away.

"Why don't you go speak to your wife"

In a shadowed corner of the camp, Jo — the grizzled 62-year-old militant with tired eyes and a rusted machete — sat alone. He was drinking again. The palm wine had returned to his breath, his fingers stained with old oil and shame. He muttered to himself as he cleaned his blade, though it had nothing left to sharpen.

Jo had once fought for purpose — for the wife he'd lost to an oil spill, for a future where Tombia wasn't a poisoned swamp. But now, he fought out of habit. And when night came, he rowed out of camp — alone, through the mangroves — to a dockside bar in Okigwe.

No one followed.

No one noticed.

At the bar, he found comfort in silence, in old jazz from the radio, in the company of strangers who didn't know he was part of Nzali. He met a woman there — Amara, soft-spoken, curious, thirty-something with warm eyes and a perfect memory.

They drank together.

She asked questions, small ones.

He answered too much.

And when he slept beside her, the sleeve of his shirt slipped, revealing a tattoo: a clenched fist wrapped around a machete.

Amara memorised it.

She was Joint Task Force.

And Jo never knew.

Back in the creek camp, Isabelle plotted Nzali's next strike.

"A convoy," she told Priye, unfurling a satellite image.

"Government tankers moving oil west. Two Humvees. Thirty men. We hit them hard. No survivors."

Priye didn't answer immediately.

"What if we take prisoners? Send a message."

"No," she said. "This isn't about negotiation. It's about fear."

He stared at her.

"You're not Tonye."

She met his gaze.

"Exactly."

On Isabelle's orders, King Emekuku's daughter — taken during the palace raid — was returned to the village.

It wasn't mercy, It was strategy.

Ebi drove the truck herself, the girl gagged and blindfolded in the back. When they reached Okigwe Market, she pulled her out by the arm and threw her to the crowd.

"Tell your father we're watching," Ebi spat.

"Now run."

The girl stumbled forward, barefoot, sobbing.

The king's daughter collapsed into her father's arms hours later.

"They are watching us" she whispered. "Though they were nice to me, but next time it could be worse. I would be leaving for Lagos at first light"

King Emekuku stood on the palace steps the next day, trying to speak to his people.

"We seek peace!" he shouted.

"Nzali cannot be our future!"

But no one stayed to hear him. Even the wind had stopped listening.

The ambush happened at dawn. Thirty Nzali fighters moved like phantoms through the swamp — boots light, weapons oiled, minds sharpened. Explosives detonated the first tanker in a fireball. Snipers picked off the soldiers as they scrambled for cover.

By the time the second Humvee exploded, the road was painted in smoke and screaming.

Priye led from the front — jaw tight, eyes empty.

He hurled a grenade through the last windshield, the explosion throwing bodies like dolls.

"This is Nzali!" he roared.

The jungle answered with silence.

Later that afternoon, reports reached Abuja.

"Convoy destroyed. No survivors. Video footage confirmed."

The President's hand trembled on his desk.

U.N. alerts sounded. Oil stocks tanked. Panic spread.

Nzali wasn't fading.

Nzali was rising again.

At the site of the convoy attack, Hawk stood among the twisted wreckage.

Blood pooled around charred tires. Flies buzzed.

"They're escalating," he muttered to Henry Ofili.

"They're not rebels anymore. They're something worse."

But Henry shook his head.

"No," he said.

"They're something different. And we're always one step behind."

Hawk looked out across the burning highway.

"Not next time."

Later that night, Priye crept into Isabelle's tent —
Tonye's knife in hand.

She was awake. Waiting.

"You killed him," he said quietly.

"Didn't you?"

She didn't flinch.

"Nzali lives because I act. Not because I grieve."

He raised the knife — then stopped.

And turned away.

"If you ever cross me again…." he whispered.

Then he left.
But the doubt had already taken root.

CHAPTER 8:
THE REFINERY GAMBIT

The heat returned to the Niger Delta like vengeance. The rains had passed. The air turned thick and sharp again, heavy with mosquitoes and the scent of rotting algae. But in Nzali's creek camp, the dominant scent now was gun oil, diesel, and a slow-burning hunger for escalation.

Weeks had passed since Tonye's death. The camp was quieter — not in mourning, but in limbo. Tonye had been the fire. Now, the ashes smouldered. Nzali hadn't unravelled, but it had hardened — moving with the cold resolve of an organisation no longer fuelled by emotion, but by calculation.

Isabelle stepped fully into that vacuum. With Priye still distant and grieving, she consolidated leadership behind the scenes: command chains reinforced, cache points secured, alliances renewed. Even the older lieutenants — men once loyal only to Priye — began to defer to her authority.

And now, she was ready to act again.

Inside the strategy hut, she hovered over a laminated satellite image of the Rivers Refinery Complex. It was one of the most heavily protected energy assets in southern Nigeria — pipelines, loading depots, administrative towers, and tanks that fed crude into ships for export.

"We're not just burning oil," she told the few assembled officers. "We're rewriting who holds the match."

Her voice was low but steely.

Priye stood nearby, silent. He listened, but his thoughts were elsewhere — caught between the weight of Tonye's knife on his belt and the suspicion that the war had changed shape in ways he no longer controlled.

Nzali's ranks had shifted too.

Younger recruits called Isabelle The Mind of the Creek. New chants carried her name alongside the brotherhood's. She didn't seek adoration, but it followed her. Only Jo — the grizzled elder — ever spoke against her influence, and even then, only after too much palm wine. No one listened anymore.

Meanwhile, Kabor had returned word.

Nzali's mole within the offshore oil systems of the Nigerian government — loyal, careful, still unseen — sent confirmation: he had secured a foreign buyer.

A man named **Albert Dimitri**.

An American. Former expatriate. Former oil sector strategist who had once worked in Nigeria during pipeline expansions a decade earlier. That's when he'd met Kabor — a young logistics officer at the time. Now, Kabor described him as quiet, curious... and dangerous. The kind of man who didn't ask what you were selling — just how much and how soon.

More than that: Kabor had provided coordinates. A private dock off Boma Island. Payment would come through layered shell accounts, and crypto. Ammunitions and supplies to be picked-up from the same location as part-payment. The buyers would never see Nzali. And Nzali would never meet Dimitri in person.

It was ideal.

Clean. Deniable. Scalable.

The timing couldn't be better.

Isabelle presented the refinery strike as more than just sabotage.

"This is our smokescreen," she said. "While the government scrambles to contain the backlash, we move the shipment. The chaos will cover our tracks."

The plan required precision. Multiple teams:

- **Team A** would cut power and breach the perimeter gate.
- **Team B** would plant C4 along the feeder pipelines.
- **Team C**, led by Priye, would target the crude tanks — the economic heart of the facility.

The move was bold. Risky. But they'd done worse with less.

They set off at night — forty fighters, faces smeared with black clay, clothes soaked in swamp water and silence.

The refinery's security was intense. Motion sensors, armed guards, roaming vehicles. But Kabor's intelligence had mapped everything.

At 00:41 hours, Team A neutralised the east gate. Silent blades. Two guards down. Power lines severed.

At 00:49, Team B entered through the drainage culvert, planting explosives along the pipeline intake.

At 01:03, Priye led his team across the upper catwalk toward the main tank yard.

It was there, under moonlight and sulphur sky, that he felt Tonye's absence most. This would've been his kind of fight — loud, reckless, historic. But Priye wasn't here for legacy.

He was here for **leverage**.

At 01:17, the first explosion shattered the calm.

The northeast valve station erupted in a fireball — a scream of metal and smoke. Seconds later, secondary charges blew through the pipeline trench, rupturing the feeder lines.

Then came the tanks.

One… then two… then a domino of pressure ruptures lit the southern block of the refinery.

The sky turned orange.

The smoke spread into the township within minutes.

Nzali didn't wait to watch it burn.

They vanished back into the water, moving as shadows into mangrove veins.

In Port Harcourt, government officials scrambled. Emergency lines flooded. Helicopters lifted. Newsrooms spun.

The refinery blaze was declared the **worst energy sabotage in over two decade**.

Oil futures plummeted.

International alerts were issued.

Markets reeled.

And in the confusion — Nzali moved the cargo.

Just before dawn, three fishing boats left the mouth of the Bonny River. Each disguised, each lined with industrial drums sealed tight. No flags. No radios. Only whispered coordinates and a moonless tide.

They docked six hours later at the edge of Boma Island — a forgotten inlet near a decommissioned customs post.

Waiting there: Dimitri's crew. Unmarked trucks. Anonymous handlers. Faces hidden behind mirrored sunglasses and clipped European accents.

No conversation. Just barrels offloaded, scanned, verified.

Encrypted tokens and ammunitions exchanged.

Digital transfer initiated.

Back at the creek, Isabelle sat at her laptop. The offshore account pinged.

Payment received. Full. Clean.

She turned to Priye.

"It's done. Our oil is in Europe. Paid in full."

He didn't reply.

Just stared at the flame of the lantern between them. They weren't rebels anymore. They were **players**.

And they had just banked their first major **war dividend**.

CHAPTER 9:
THE DELTA'S RECKONING

At dawn, the mangroves were still.

Not with peace — but with anticipation.

Birdsong had fallen silent. Smoke from the refinery still loomed faint in the distance. The entire region held its breath, waiting for the next crack of thunder.

The Joint Task Force compound in Port Harcourt was in full lockdown. Steel gates sealed. Antennas buzzed. Inside the control centre, Steven "Hawk" Caldwell stood at the centre of the war table, helmet under one arm, eyes on the satellite map blinking red. He wasn't pacing anymore. He was ready.

Beside him, Nosa Badmus, Nigeria's director of special operations, was grim and silent. The recent failure to prevent the refinery attack had stung. His face was tight with shame and fury.

"They humiliated us," Nosa said.

Hawk nodded. "Then we make sure they don't get another chance."

Henry Ofili, the tactical analyst, reviewed the updated drone feeds of Nzali's creek camp. "We've got full visual. Camp perimeter lit. Armoury, boatyard, watch-posts. Looks like they're rotating shifts every three hours. But they don't expect a ground incursion this soon."

"They expect fear," Hawk replied. "Let's give them war instead."

The order was simple.

No delays. No mercy.

Nzali's bold refinery attack had forced their hand.

They were done waiting.

They called it the final push — but in truth, it was retaliation.

A reckoning.

Hawk's team launched before dusk — two battalions split across riverine assault crafts and overland units, flanking the camp from east and south. A third group approached from the mangrove wall, using sniper scouts and drone heat mapping to track escape routes.

With approval from Aso Rock, **Operation Backwater** was in motion.

Its purpose was clear:

Neutralise Nzali. Permanently.

What no one knew was that the breach had already begun days earlier. The leak came from within.

Jo. Nzali's oldest militant. The one with the cracked machete and the oil-stained past. Weary, lonely, and searching for something he couldn't name.

He had wandered into Okigwe again one night — into the arms of Amara, the woman who asked nothing and listened to everything.

Amara, who touched his wrist when he spoke.

Who noticed the tattoo under his sleeve.

Who handed him one more drink before he passed out.

She worked for the JTF.

By the time Jo awoke, the information was already in the system. Coordinates. Patterns. Schedules. Names.

They didn't even need to break him. He gave them everything.

Unwittingly. Tragically.

Enough to burn a revolution to the ground.

At the creek camp, Priye stood at the dock in the early light, eyes on the water, hand wrapped around Tonye's knife.

He sensed it. Not in any radio static or lookouts' reports — but in his gut. Something had shifted. The silence was too sharp.

He called for Isabelle.

They stood alone in the command hut.

"They're coming," he said.

Her jaw clenched.

"We're not prepared."

"No," he replied. "We're exposed."

She moved fast.

"Take the command team to fallback. Get the backups. Trigger the tunnel."

"You won't make it."

"I'll try."

She didn't ask him to leave.

He didn't offer to stay.

They were soldiers. Not lovers. Not anymore.

As explosions rocked the eastern watchpoint, they split.

The first wave hit like a hammer.

Mortars pounded the barracks. Sniper fire cut down three guards before they fired a shot. Drone-guided missiles struck the armoury, igniting caches of ammunition in a blast that echoed across the Delta.

Nzali fighters scrambled.

But the JTF were trained. Coordinated. Backed by American tech and Nigerian intelligence.

It wasn't a raid, It was a purge.

Priye fought until he bled.

He moved through the camp like a ghost — picking off flanking troops, shouting orders, dragging the wounded to cover.

He didn't run. He didn't call for surrender. He just kept firing.

Until they overran the main hut and Hawk's boots landed in the dirt behind him.

"On your knees."

Priye turned — eyes red with smoke, chest heaving.

"You think this ends it?"

"No," Hawk said. "But it ends you."

They cuffed him. Threw a black hood over his head.

And dragged the commander of Nzali away from the ashes of his camp.

Elsewhere, in the mangrove tunnel, Isabelle limped through the darkness, one hand pressed against a bleeding shoulder.

Ebi was with her. They reached the halfway point before they heard pursuit — boots splashing, voices shouting in American accents.

Ebi turned.

"No," Isabelle said.

Ebi pressed the remote into her hand.

"You have to go."

"You won't make it."

Ebi smiled. "Not planning to."

She turned, faced the darkness, and detonated the charge.

The tunnel collapsed behind her in a roar of fire and earth — sealing the path, crushing the walls, and burying Ebi beneath tonnes of mud and stone.

She died in the blast. A soldier to the end.

Isabelle surfaced in the outer channel two hours later, covered in mud and blood. She climbed into a hidden canoe. Started paddling. Behind her, Nzali was smoke.

Ahead, only silence.

And opportunity.

Back in Tombia, the villagers awoke to military sirens, overhead rotors, and the smell of scorched earth.

The king didn't panic.

He didn't weep. Instead, he walked out to the square at midday, gathered the community, and raised his voice.

"I was meant to protect you. To speak for you. I failed."

He removed the beaded crown from his head.

"I cannot be king any longer."

He placed it on the stone bench beside the marketplace. Then turned and walked into the crowd.

No guards.

No farewell.

Just a man, fading into his people.

A relic stepping away from history.

Nzali's camp was razed.

Its fighters were scattered.

Its leaders either captured, presumed dead, or vanished.

But its legacy…

That could not be burned.

In the mission chapel, Sister Maria lit a candle for Priye.

One for Tonye.

And one more — for whatever still pulsed in the swamp that the world hadn't yet named.

The rosary trembled in her fingers, but she didn't stop praying.

She never would.

EPILOGUE:
THE RIVER WILL RISE AGAIN

The Niger-Delta was quiet.

Not peaceful — never peaceful — but hushed. Like a battlefield after the last shot, where the smoke curls slowly and the vultures circle wide. The mangroves held their breath, and the creeks ran slow, heavy with oil, ash, and memory.

Nzali was gone.

Its camp — burned.

Its men — scattered.

Its name — etched into Nigeria's darkest headlines and whispered fears.

But the story hadn't ended.

Not yet.

Abuja.

A pale sun clawed its way above the horizon, spilling sickly light over the maximum-security yard where two men stood facing a blank concrete wall.

Priye Mazani.

His shoulders bandaged, his wrists shackled, his beard coarse and unkempt — a shadow of the commander he once was.

Jo.

Battered, sunken-eyed, and hollow. A man who had once swung a machete for Nzali and now barely had the strength to stand.

The guard barked orders.

Boots echoed on gravel.

An execution squad lined up — rifles in hand, faces unreadable.

Sister Maria had been requested by Priye himself — not out of faith, but familiarity. In the shadow of death, he wanted one face that knew his story, one voice that had witnessed the road that led him there.

The captain called out:

"Ready—"

Then—

Chaos.

Sirens tore through the silence like teeth.

A convoy of unmarked black SUVs exploded through the outer gates.

Doors slammed.

Men in black suits and body armour swarmed the compound like hornets.

Secret Service.

Their commander strode forward, voice like steel:

"STAND DOWN!"

"Presidential order!"

The execution squad froze, rifles trembling mid-air.

The captain stepped forward, confused, eyes darting — until a gloved hand thrust a sealed envelope into his chest.

The red seal of the presidency glared up at him.

The captain tore it open.

Read once.

Read again.

He stepped back and lowered his weapon.

"Execution… is cancelled."

No one spoke.

Not the guards.

Not the prisoners.

Jo let out a single breath — more a gasp than a laugh — and looked skyward, whispering:

"Maybe… the river does remember."

Priye didn't move.

Not a blink. Not a sound.
But deep in his chest, something cold twisted.

Later that day, they were dragged back to their cells.

No answers were given.
No explanations.

Just silence.

Until the warden arrived with two soldiers and a new letter.

He read it aloud, slowly, like he didn't quite believe it himself:

"By executive order…
These men are to be transported to **No-Man's Island**.
To remain there for the rest of their natural lives."

"Death," the president wrote in a margin, "is too easy."

No-Man's Island.

Few had heard the name.

Fewer still had seen it.

A forgotten black rock floating in a corner of the Gulf where no map dared label it.

The water surrounding it churned with crocodiles.

The beaches were lined with mines.

The inner land riddled with booby traps older than the men who would be buried by them.

No one ever escaped.

One way in.
No way out.

No visitors.
No communication.
No light — save the moon.

A place where prisoners grew what they ate.

And when the crops failed…
They fed on the dead.

Back in Tombia, life crept forward.

The markets reopened.

Children played again by the riverbanks.

But the air held a weight it hadn't before.

Sister Maria, now back in Tombia**,** walked barefoot through what remained of her chapel — now just stone, ash, and memory.

She lit three candles each night.

One for **Tonye**.

One for **Priye**.

One for the **Delta** — for everything that was stolen and everything still left to protect.

A child once asked about the Nzali flag scorched into the dirt.

Maria knelt, pressed her palm to it.

"They were boys once," she whispered.
"Before the guns. Before the greed. Before we failed them."

Albert Dimitri vanished.

Offshore accounts — gone.

Offices — abandoned.

Interpol hunted. The Americans denied him.

A customs officer swore they saw him boarding a freighter in Marseille under a different name.

No one could prove it.

No one really wanted to.

And then, the signs returned.

A clenched machete painted on a derelict church wall in Bayelsa.

A slogan scrawled in blood-red across a refugee tent in Ghana.

A hacked JTF transmission from Warri's oil corridor.

Fourteen seconds.

"The river remembers."

And **Isabelle**?

No satellite ever tracked her.

No drone ever spotted her.

No corpse ever washed ashore.

The bounty remained untouched.

Some say she drowned — claimed by the river goddess.
Others say she escaped to the Congo.

A whisper. A ghost. A myth in combat boots.

But nobody knew.

Not yet.

And so, the Delta quieted… but never healed.

Because Nzali was never just a militia.

It was a **message**.

It was a **memory**.

It was a match tossed into a leaking pipeline.

And though its leaders were buried — in silence, in shame, in the belly of the earth—

The Delta still whispered.

And in that whisper:

Nzali breathes.
Nzali waits.
Nzali will rise again.

BONUS CHAPTER:
MARIA

They arrived in Tombia during the wet season —

her parents wide-eyed and willing,

their suitcases swollen with medicine, Bibles, and old good intentions.

Maria was just eight.

Too young to know what sacrifice meant, but old enough to notice the stares.

She stood between her mother's stiff smile and her father's camera lens, clutching a tin lunchbox with one name scratched into the lid:

Maria.

They weren't missionaries in the traditional sense.

Not clergy. Not ordained.

Just volunteers — one of the many families that had joined the European team to help expand the Christian mission in the Niger-Delta.

Mother Elizabeth was already there when they arrived.

Tall. Weathered. Quiet.

She wore a black habit and carried a silence that made people listen.

Maria noticed how the locals nodded at Elizabeth with cautious respect.

How she didn't preach. She simply stayed.

Unlike the others, she never flinched at the sound of distant gunfire.

And she never spoke of going back.

Maria was drawn to her instantly.

When her parents were busy distributing pamphlets or arguing about power cuts, Maria followed Elizabeth.

She swept the chapel floors.

Cleaned lanterns.

Learned how to pray without speaking.

Elizabeth treated her like a daughter — long before the world forced that bond to become real.

Then came the sickness.

Malaria. Cholera. Dysentery.

Death crept into the guts like mist.

One by one, the other missionaries began to fall ill.

Some recovered. Others didn't.

The ones who could still stand began to panic. Rumours of the **gods of the village** fighting back had spread around the chapel.

They called for boats, packed their trunks in the dark, and prayed quick, shallow prayers.

Maria's parents were among them — frantic, confused, already half-packed when the call came to evacuate.

In the chaos of loading and counting, amid coughing and shouting, someone told them Maria had already gone ahead with a family friend to the boats.

They believed it.

They left.

She never saw them again.

And no one came back for her.

Elizabeth stayed.

She found Maria crying in the storage room behind the chapel, clutching a sandal and staring at the door.

They never spoke about it.

There was no comfort to offer.

Only survival.

They buried the dead.

Washed the sick.

And started again.

With time, Maria stopped waiting for someone to return.

She worked.

She cleaned.

She learned to pray in silence — long, slow prayers that settled into the bones.

The chapel became her home.

It was during the quietest of months that **Tonye and Priye** arrived.

Or rather, were found.

Two teenage boys scavenging behind the market — thin, wild, silent.

Born of pain — their mother a casualty of violence, their father unknown.

They didn't beg.
They didn't trust.
But they followed Mother Elizabeth back to the chapel because she offered them bread without questions.

They were like her in ways she couldn't explain.

Abandoned, but unbroken.
Lost, but watching.

She taught them how to hold a rosary.

How to read slow English from a battered Psalms book.

She hoped — quietly, deeply — that they would grow into men of faith.

She imagined them as priests once.

Saw in them a future she never dared name aloud.

But the world had other plans.

Mother Elizabeth grew frail.

The Delta darkened.

And the boys she loved became leaders of a militia with blood on their hands.

Still, Maria stayed.

She never left the chapel.

She kept the candles burning — not for what was, but for what might still be saved.

One for **Elizabeth**.

One for **the boys**.

And one for **the river**, which forgets nothing and forgives rarely.

DEDICATION

To the people of the **Niger-Delta** —

To the fishermen whose nets come up heavy with oil.

To the mothers whose children cough in silence.

To the villages drowned not by flood, but by forgotten promises.

To every voice unheard, every life undervalued, every soul left waiting.

This story is for you.

May the world see your truth.

May justice find your shores.

And may your spirit — like the river —

Never stop flowing.

ABOUT THE AUTHOR

Michael Kallys is a British entrepreneur and writer originally from Nigeria. Raised between two worlds — the humid oil towns of the Niger-Delta and the structured streets of Glasgow — his storytelling blends the visceral urgency of West African realities with the pacing and grit of modern thrillers.

With a background in business and a lifelong passion for narrative justice, Michael writes to spotlight the people and places often left in the margins. Nzali: The Brotherhood is his debut novel — a raw, emotionally charged story about rebellion, survival, and what happens when silence becomes unbearable.

The novel draws inspiration from real tensions in the Niger-Delta: environmental devastation, government neglect, and the human cost of global greed. But at its core, it is a story about brotherhood, betrayal, and hope in the face of impossible odds.

When he's not writing, Michael draws inspiration from family, music, history, and the enduring tension between survival and dignity. He believes in the power of fiction to unearth truth — and in the power of truth to spark change.

He lives in the U.K with his wife and children, and is currently working on the next book in the Nzali series.

ACKNOWLEDGEMENTS

Writing this novel has been a journey of years — filled with starts, stops, rewrites, and revelations. I am deeply grateful to my wife, Deborah Kallys, whose patience, faith, and quiet strength have carried me through the hardest parts of this process. To my children, Safaree and Deltaa, for reminding me every day why stories matter.

Thank you to the readers, early listeners, and quiet believers who encouraged me to finish this. To the communities whose struggles inspired this story — I hope this work honours your resilience.

And finally, to anyone fighting for justice in a world that doesn't always reward it — **this book is for you**.

Printed in Great Britain
by Amazon